FRANKLY, I'D RATHER
SPIN MYSELF A NEW NAME!

The Story of
RUMPELSTILTSKIN as Told by
RUMPELSTILTSKIN

by Jessica Gunderson

illustrated by Janna Bock

PICTURE WINDOW BOOKS
a capstone imprint

Special thanks to our adviser, Terry Flaherty, PhD, Professor of English,
Minnesota State University, Mankato, for his expertise.

⌁⌁⌁

Editor: Jill Kalz
Designer: Ted Williams
Creative Director: Nathan Gassman
Production Specialist: Jennifer Walker
The illustrations in this book were created digitally.

⌁⌁⌁

Picture Window Books
1710 Roe Crest Drive
North Mankato, MN 56003
www.mycapstone.com

Library of Congress Cataloging-in-Publication Data
Cataloging-in-publication information is on file with the Library of Congress.
ISBN 978-1-4795-8624-0 (library binding)
ISBN 978-1-4795-8628-8 (paperback)
ISBN 978-1-4795-8632-5 (eBook PDF)

Printed and bound in the USA.
062017 010565R

My name is Rumpelstiltskin. I know, I know ... Horrible name, isn't it? Impossible to spell. I'm not sure what my mother was thinking when she gave it to me. Thankfully she always called me "Al." So did everyone else. I thought I could keep my real name a secret forever.

Boy was I wrong ...

Let me start at the beginning. I'm a traveling gold-spinner. I go door to door all around the kingdom and spin straw into gold. It's not hard, really. All it takes is a bit of science and a lot of practice. People pay me oodles of cash.

Everyone loves gold.

One day as I was passing by the king's castle, I heard someone crying. I poked my head through an open window. Inside, on a pile of straw, sat a young maiden.

"What's wrong?" I asked.

"The king ordered me to spin this straw into gold!" she wailed. **"If I don't, I'll die!"**

"You're in luck," I said. "I know how. But my skill has a price."

"I can pay you with my necklace," the maiden said.

I would've rather had cash, but I accepted.

While I worked, the maiden told me a long story about her father. He was poor and wanted to look important, so he told the king his daughter could turn straw into gold. (She can't.) When I finished spinning, the maiden gave me her necklace, and away I went.

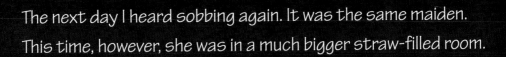

The next day I heard sobbing again. It was the same maiden. This time, however, she was in a much bigger straw-filled room.

"The king was ever so pleased with the gold," she said, "but now he wants even more! And if I don't spin all of this—"

"OK, OK," I said. "What will you give me if I help you?"

"I can pay you with my ring," she said.

So I spun the straw into gold, took the ring, and went home.

The following afternoon I heard the maiden weeping **AGAIN**.
She sat in an enormous room packed wall-to-wall, floor-to-ceiling
with straw. The king would marry her, she explained, if she spun
all the straw into gold.

"I beg you to help me, dear sir," she said. "I want to be queen, but
I have nothing left to give you."

That's when I got to thinking. I'd always wanted kids. But I didn't have a girlfriend or a wife. I traveled too much. Plus I'd have to put my real name on a marriage license, and I didn't want to do that.

"You can pay me later," I told the maiden. **"How about your firstborn son?"**

"Yes, of course. I'll give you anything!" she said.

I spun every last bit of straw in that room into gold. Then I went back to my cottage and thought about what a great dad I'd be someday.

Life went on. I traveled far and wide,
spinning straw until my fingers hurt.
About a year later, I returned home.

14

Newspapers had piled up on my doorstep. Right on top was a picture of the maiden (now the queen) holding a super-cute baby.

"Woohoo!" I cried. **Time to collect my payment.**

KING
QUEE.
NEW I
BOY!

15

The queen looked surprised to see me. "What was your name again?" she asked.

I ignored the question and asked for the baby.

"Certainly not!" she said.

I reminded her of her promise. But she just hugged the baby tightly and babbled on about feeding times and teething pains and how she loved her boy and couldn't give him up ... blah, blah, blah.

"Fine," I said. "Guess my real name in three days, and you can keep your baby. I'll warn you, it's very unusual."

"I've got it!" the queen told me the next day. "Your name is **Caspar!**"

I shook my head.

"Melchior?"

"Nope."

"Balthazar? Ichabod? Ulysses?"

"Uh-uh," I said.

The second day she guessed, **"Sheep-shank? Ribs-of-beef? Leg of lamb?"**

"No," I said. "Not even close. Tomorrow's your last chance."

That night I danced with glee. The queen would
never guess my name. I even sang a little song.
"Ho, ho, ho, only I know! Hear my laugh?
See my grin? My name is Rumpelstiltskin!"

On the third day, the queen asked, "Is your name Puffernut? Lump-a-glump? Smear-and-sheer? Lollypoodle?"

"Very creative," I told her. "But no."

She smiled. "Is it ... **RUMPELSTILTSKIN?**"

My jaw dropped. "It's not possible! How in the world did you ever ... What ARE you—a mind reader?"

She grinned and cuddled her baby.

What a bummer! What about the toys I'd bought?
The nursery I'd painted? I stamped my foot hard, and
it went right through the floor. When I tried to pull it
out, my leg came off. **IT CAME OFF!**

21

I did learn a couple important lessons from my adventure:
Get paid right away, and take only cash.

The worst part? Now everyone calls me Rumpelstiltskin instead of Al. My secret's out. And I can't fit my name on my business cards. Although I guess it's still better to be called Rumpelstiltskin than Lollypoodle, right?

Critical Thinking Using the Common Core

Rumpelstiltskin preferred cash for his work. But what other kinds of payment did he accept? (Key Ideas and Details)

Look online to find the original "Rumpelstiltskin" story. Describe how Rumpelstiltskin looks and acts. Compare and contrast that Rumpelstiltskin to the one in this version of the story. (Integration of Knowledge and Ideas)

The king doesn't appear as a character in this version, but we hear of him through the maiden. Try telling the story from the king's point of view. What details might he not know? (Craft and Structure)

Glossary

character—a person, animal, or creature in a story
plot—what happens in a story
point of view—a way of looking at something
version—an account of something from a certain point of view

Read More

Charles, Veronika Martenova. *It's Not About the Straw!* Easy-to-Read Wonder Tales. Plattsburgh, N.Y.: Tundra Books, 2013.

Pearson, Maggie. *Rumpelstiltskin Returns.* Race Ahead with Reading. New York: Crabtree Publishing Company, 2015.

Shurtliff, Liesl. *Rump: The True Story of Rumpelstiltskin.* New York: Alfred A. Knopf, 2013.

Internet Sites

FactHound offers a safe, fun way to find Internet sites related to this book. All of the sites on FactHound have been researched by our staff.

Here's all you do:
Visit *www.facthound.com*
Type in this code: 9781479586240

Look for all the books in the series:

Believe Me, Goldilocks Rocks!

Believe Me, I Never Felt a Pea!

Frankly, I'd Rather Spin Myself a New Name!

Frankly, I Never Wanted to Kiss Anybody!

Honestly, Red Riding Hood Was Rotten!

No Kidding, Mermaids Are a Joke!

No Lie, I Acted Like a Beast!

No Lie, Pigs (and Their Houses) CAN Fly!

Really, Rapunzel Needed a Haircut!

Seriously, Cinderella Is SO Annoying!

Seriously, Snow White Was SO Forgetful!

Truly, We Both Loved Beauty Dearly!

Trust Me, Hansel and Gretel Are SWEET!

Trust Me, Jack's Beanstalk Stinks!

Super-cool stuff!

Check out projects, games and lots more at
www.capstonekids.com